Fashion Fairy
Princess

Thanks fairy much Catherine Coe!

First published in the UK in 2014 by Scholastic Children's Books
An imprint of Scholastic Ltd
Euston House, 24 Eversholt Street
London, NW1 1DB, UK
Registered office: Westfield Road, Southam, Warwickshire, CV47 0RA
SCHOLASTIC and associated logos are trademarks and/or registered
trademarks of Scholastic Inc.

ISBN 978 1407 14587 7

A CIP catalogue record for this book is available from the British Library.

Printed and bound by CPI Group (UK) Ltd, Croydon, CR0 4YY
Papers used by Scholastic Children's Books are made
from wood grown in sustainable forests.

1 3 5 7 9 10 8 6 4 2

www.scholastic.co.uk
www.fashionfairyprincess.com

Fashion Fairy Princess

Blossom
in Jewel Forest

POPPY COLLINS

SCHOLASTIC

Dream
Mountain

Jewel Forest

Sparkle
City

Star
Valley

River
Sapphire

Shimmer Island

Glitter Ocean

Welcome to the world of the fashion fairy princesses! Join Blossom and friends on their magical adventures in fairyland.

They can't wait to explore

Jewel Forest!

Can you?

Chapter 1

Blossom was pulling the latest tray of diamond-glitter brownies out of the bakery oven when she heard the door open and a little voice call out.

"Hi, Blossom, are you there?"

Blossom popped up her head from behind the counter and saw Pip standing in the doorway, waving and smiling. Her tiny forest fairy friend wore a gorgeous fern grass dress with

matching dangly earrings. Blossom
looked down at herself. She had icing
sugar all over her tights, dandelion flour
covered her apron, and she was certain
she had cake mixture stuck in her
unruly blonde hair!

"Oh, hello, Pip.
I'm sorry I look
such a mess!
It's all been
a bit crazy
getting ready
for the Jewel Forest
fête tomorrow."

Everyone loved the
annual fête. Fairies
came from all over
fairyland to join in the
fun and games – and to sample Blossom's
famous cakes!

"I thought it might be, so I wanted to pop in and see how you were doing," said Pip. "You mustn't work too hard, you know."

"But the cake sale is the highlight of the fête!" Blossom took a tray of unbaked muffins from the counter and slid them into the steaming hot oven. She threw in some more fairy-dust to keep up the temperature. "All the cakes have to be perfect!"

Pip looked around the bakery. Every single surface was covered. There were open bags of flour and sugar, cake stands in beautiful pastel colours, biscuits cooling, fairy buns with their icing setting, and bowls of mixture waiting to be put into moulds. She wondered whether Blossom would get everything done in time, but she didn't want to ask and risk hurting her friend's feelings. Blossom was the best baker in the forest, after all.

"While the muffins are baking, let me show you some of my cake designs," Blossom suggested, fluttering around the counter and heading towards the walnut table where customers usually sat. Today that would have been impossible, as it was covered in cake boxes – some already made, some still flat and waiting to be put together.

Pip moved a pile of unmade cake boxes from a chair and placed them carefully on the floor while Blossom grabbed a large daisy-paper scrapbook from the window sill.

"I've been working on the recipe for the moonbutter cakes for weeks," said Blossom, pointing to a pencil drawing of cupcakes with butter icing in the shape of crescent moons.

"Oh, they look delicious!" Pip peered at the scrapbook. Blossom's drawings were so detailed she could almost taste them!

Blossom turned a page. "And this is how I've designed the diamond-glitter brownies. When they're put on to their cake stand, they'll look like a sparkling tree trunk!"

"What a great idea – and perfect for a forest fête," agreed Pip.

"Thanks, Pip," said Blossom, grinning.
"And let me show you what I'm
planning for the highlight of my
stall. . ." Blossom flicked through the
pages with her dough-covered fingers.
"Here it is – the double-layer sunshine
cake!"

A huge two-layer cake had been
drawn on the page, with shimmering rays
bursting out of the top. "It will be iced

with edible jewels straight from the Jewel
Tree, which will shoot rays of sunshine
from the cake as you eat it. It's going
to be very special — I hope so, anyway."
The Jewel Tree was the first tree ever to
grow in the forest and the source of all
the forest fairy magic. Blossom closed the
scrapbook and jumped up. "I must check
on the muffins!"

She whizzed behind the bakery counter
and opened the oven. Mouth-watering
smells flooded the whole room with
chocolatey-sugar sweetness. Pip breathed
in deeply. "Mmmmm, yum!"

"Um, Pip, could you hold these a
moment while I put the ruby-jam tarts in
the oven?" Blossom asked.

"Of course!" Pip put on a spare pair
of moss-stitch oven gloves that had been
hanging on the wall and took the tray of

muffins from Blossom. She looked at the cooling counter, and saw there was no room whatsoever for another tray.

The counter was covered in freshly baked goodies, waiting for icing or decorations, or to be filled with cream. She worried again that her friend had taken on more than she could handle. She took a deep breath. "Er, Blossom . . . are you going to be OK with all of this? I mean, will you really get it done in time?"

Blossom looked up at her friend from

where she crouched beside the oven door. "Of course!" She glanced around the bakery – she knew there was a lot to do, but she was sure she'd manage.

"And anyway, the whole forest is relying on me! I can't let them down."

"The cakes will be delicious, I know it. But I'd better go now." Pip held up an empty dress bag. "I was on my way to pick up my fancy dress for the fête competition!"

"Ooh, how exciting – what are you going as?" asked Blossom as she filled a piping bag with honey-cream.

"Now that's a secret!" Pip winked. "But I'll give you a clue: it'll be *berry* special!"

"Oh, that reminds me – I haven't collected the blackberries for the fairy-fruit four-layer cupcakes yet!" Blossom grabbed a large purple-straw basket from a rose-thorn hook on the wall, then untied her apron and popped it on the hook. "I'd better go now – there won't be any time later. I'll come with you!"

Chapter 2

Outside was just as frantic as inside the bakery. Along the fairy skyway – leafy bridges high above the forest floor – hundreds of pointy-eared forest fairies rushed around, many of them carrying baskets or sacks slung over their shoulders. It seemed as if the entire forest was preparing for the fête the next day.

Pretty pink hummingbirds busily hung up leaf bunting with their beaks along the sparkling railings of the skyway. Jewel moths zoomed about carrying web-silk, and ants scuttled back and forth with fête lanterns on their back. Blossom and Pip were so busy taking everything in, their mouths open in awe, that at first they didn't hear Primrose – not until the fairy princess tapped on their shoulders.

"Blossom, Pip! I thought it was you," said Primrose as the two fairies swung round. The princess's arms were full of beautifully wrapped presents. "I'm just on my way to drop off these raffle prizes! What are you up to?"

Blossom held up her basket. "I need to collect blackberries for some of my cakes," she said.

"And I'm going to pick up my fancy-dress outfit from the tailor's," Pip said in her small voice. "I can't wait for you to see it!"

"Neither can I," said Primrose, beaming. "And I can't wait to see your stall, Blossom – I'm going to make sure I'm hungry so I can try as many treats as possible! Everyone at the Tree Palace has been talking about your cakes. They're longing to taste them! How is the baking going? You must have so much to do."

Blossom nodded. "But it's all under control!" she said. "I have lots to do today, but that's always the way with baking – if I want the cakes to be their freshest, most things have to be prepared at the last minute!"

"I should let you go, then," said Primrose. "Good luck with everything!" The fairy princess fluttered away, weighed down with the raffle prizes.

"I'll leave you here, too, Blossom," said Pip. "I must hurry to Starlight-Starbright tailor's."

Blossom clapped a hand to her forehead, her cheeks turning pink. "Oh, that reminds me! The stars – I've forgotten those too!"

Pip frowned. "What do you mean?"

"I need to get star sprinkles for the glow-beam sandwich cake. Oh, I'm so glad you mentioned stars, Pip. I'll pick some up on the way back."

"I'm glad I helped! See you later, then, Blossom," called Pip in her small voice. The tiny fairy whizzed off in the opposite direction.

Blossom hurried along the fairy skyway, her mind on all the different cakes she had to finish. She almost didn't see her candy-pink tree squirrel friend, Sycamore, coming the other way. He carried so many nuts in his arms, his tufted head was barely visible above them.

"Oh, hello, Blossom," Sycamore said in his deep voice. "I'm afraid I can't stop – I've got to hide all these nuts for the Find the Nut game before sunset!"

That sounds like fun, thought Blossom. But her excitement quickly changed to a wave of panic. Sycamore had reminded her that she still needed to get walnuts for her honey and walnut tart. *It's OK*, she told herself. *I can gather some when I pick the blackberries − as long as the squirrels haven't hidden them all!*

"Good luck!" she called to Sycamore as he rushed past, his pink fluffy tail bobbing up and down.

Sycamore looked back over his shoulder at Blossom. "And good luck to you too − I can't wait to taste your cakes tomorrow!"

Blossom continued on her way, repeating over and over to herself everything she had to get while she was out. There was no time to forget anything! *Blackberries, star sprinkles,*

walnuts. . . Blackberries, star sprinkles,
walnuts. . . And she'd left the ruby-jam
tarts baking in the oven. She'd better be
quick!

Chapter 3

Blossom fell into the bakery doorway, exhausted. She carried a basket full of blackberries on one arm, a sack of walnuts slung over her shoulder, a pouch of shimmering star sprinkles in her left hand and a bunch of moth-silk in her right. The silk was another thing that had slipped her mind – as she'd left the blackberry bushes she'd bumped into another tree squirrel, Conker. He'd been

busily plaiting the tug-of-war rope, which
was made of a thousand moth-silk threads.
She'd almost forgotten that she needed
silk to tie up her cake boxes! Luckily,
Conker had lots to spare, and he'd happily
given her a few threads in exchange
for a box of ruby-jam tarts at the fête
tomorrow. Blossom knew they were his
favourite!

Blossom dropped the bags of
ingredients on the white-tiled bakery
floor. She sat down
for a moment to
catch her breath,
and felt her pale
green wings droop
with tiredness.
She closed
her eyes for
a second,

but then flashed them open, annoyed with herself. With so much to finish, there was no time to rest right now. She could do that tomorrow!

What first? she wondered, looking around. Her gaze fell on the oven – the ruby-jam tarts! Blossom jumped up and fluttered over to the oven, grabbing one of the oven mitts and yanking it open. No burning smell – *thank fairyness!* But when she pulled out the tray of tarts, she could see there was a different problem – the tarts had barely cooked at all!

Blossom looked at the bowl of fairy-dust, which she used specially to keep the oven hot. She'd forgotten to add more dust when she'd put the tarts in. She dipped her hand into the bowl, grabbed a large handful of dust and scattered it into the oven, her arms bristling with warmth as she felt the temperature increase straight away. Blossom pushed down the rising panic in her stomach and popped the tarts back in. *It's going to be OK*, she told herself.

On the counter, the mixture for the starberry muffins was laid out. Next to it stood the double-layer sunshine cake. It would be cool enough to ice with the edible jewels now. A large yellow bowl held the mixture for the glow-beam cake – that needed to be stirred, then poured into two tins ready to go in the oven. She also had to make a start on the fairy-fruit four-layer cupcakes. Her mind buzzed with all she still had to do – thinking about everything, it did seem like an awful lot of work! How had she left it all until now?

Blossom shook herself. *There's no point in worrying about it*, she thought, determined to stay positive. *I'll just have to work through the night if I have to!*

She set to work on the fairy-fruit cupcakes, pouring the fruits into four separate mixing bowls and adding some fairy flour and jewel-bee honey to each one. Making the mixture calmed her

down – baking always did – and she
hummed the sacred forest song as
she worked.

Once she'd poured each fruit layer into
the dainty orange-blossom cases, she took
the ruby-jam tarts out of the oven. They
were now crisp and golden, with the
glittering ruby-jam bubbling in the centre
of each one. *Perfect!* Blossom flew over
to the window sill to check her plans

in the scrapbook. It was dusk already so she had to light her firefly lanterns as she flicked through the pages. She turned to the one that showed the design for the moonbutter cakes — that's what she'd do next. They needed extra time to set once they'd been decorated with the butter icing.

Blossom fluttered her wings at double speed, flying back to the counter and pouring ingredients into another mixing bowl. She stirred it with a large willow-wand spoon, her arms aching as she whisked the thick batter.

Ping! went the silver-bell oven timer, telling Blossom the fairy-fruit cupcakes were ready. She opened the door once more and the delicious fruity aromas immediately filled the bakery. She set down the cupcakes, which had risen perfectly, and tested one by cutting it in half.

"Gorgeous, if I do say so myself," Blossom declared. Each layer was a different colour. A purple blackberry layer was at the bottom, and above that a green apple layer. Next was a pink strawberry layer, and on top was a yellow lemon layer. She couldn't wait for the forest fairies to try these – it was a brand new recipe! She popped one of the halves in her mouth and grinned. The fruity sponges melted on her tongue, and the flavour changed with every bite.

"OK, back to work!" Blossom told herself. She flew over to the moonbutter batter – it needed just a little more stirring before she could pour it into the cake tins. To give

her feet a rest, she sat back on a tall
kitchen toadstool as she worked. Once
the moonbutter cakes were in the oven,
she could start icing the sunshine cake.
But as the forest fairy thought of all
the things she had to do, her eyelids
began to close. Her arm stopped
mixing and her head sagged down,
until all that could be heard were her
gentle snores as she fell asleep in the
light, buttery batter.

Chapter 4

Catkin flew along the fairy skyway, her crimson wings and curly red hair shimmering in the pink sunlight. It was her favourite time of night, when dusk fell on the forest, and everything seemed even more magical than ever. Catkin was on her way to Goldie's Groceries to fetch more firelight candles for the fête – she was on the organizing committee, and in charge of lots of

things, including
the lighting.
She'd already
bought
hundreds of
candles, but
it wasn't quite
enough! Goldie had promised
to keep some reserved, just in case she
needed more. Catkin just hoped the
shop was still open!

As she fluttered along in the warm
evening air, Catkin checked off her list of
things for the fête.

Prepare the raffle tickets. ✔

Organize the extra-special raffle prize. ✔

Check the woodland decorations.

*Collect the bellflower microphone from
Toadstool Town Hall.*

Organize the tug-of-war teams.

There was a lot to do, Catkin realized, but she didn't mind. Having a late night to get everything properly prepared was worth it, to make sure the fête was spectacular!

As she approached Blossom's bakery, she noticed the lanterns were all still on. *Blossom must be working late too, finishing all the cakes for her stall*, thought Catkin. It was always one of the most popular attractions at the fête. *I wonder if she's made any starberry muffins this year?* She hoped so — they were her favourite.

Catkin reached the bakery, looked through the window and gasped. She had expected Blossom to be whizzing around the bakery as usual, but instead she was fast asleep on the counter, her blonde head lying in a puddle of batter! Catkin pressed her nose up to the glass and saw that every single surface was covered in half-finished cakes. *Poor Blossom*, she thought. *She must have been working so hard she's tired herself out.*

Catkin moved towards the closed door and reached out to open it when she stopped herself. If Blossom was this exhausted, she most definitely  needed to sleep. Rather than go inside and wake her friend, was there another way to fix this problem and help Blossom?

Catkin sat down cross-legged on

the sparkling fairy skyway. The gems
dotted over the bridge glistened in the
moonlight. Pip didn't live very far away,
in a tree house in the opal-oak tree.
Catkin leapt up and began fluttering
her crimson wings towards Pip's home.
She hoped her friend would be able to
help.

Moments later, Catkin was knocking on
the little arched door of Pip's tree house.
Because Pip was so small, everything
about her tree house was tiny too! "Pip,
are you awake?" she whispered.

Pip opened the door with a mug of
emerald-nut tea in her hand. "Hello,
Catkin, is everything all right?" Her
pretty face creased with concern when
she saw the serious look in Catkin's
eyes.

"I'm sorry to come over after nightfall,

but there's a bit of an emergency!" said
Catkin.

"That's OK!" Pip replied. "I was up
anyway, putting the finishing touches to
my fancy-dress outfit."

"Oh, I'm glad. You see, I need your
help. . ." Catkin explained to Pip how
she'd found Blossom asleep in the bakery.

Pip's eyes widened. "Oh dear! It did

seem like Blossom had an awful lot to do, but she said she'd be fine. And Blossom's always a bit disorganized, so I didn't worry too much when I saw the chaos in the bakery." She looked down. "But I feel bad – I should have realized just how hard she'd been working and how tired she was."

Catkin shook her head. "Don't worry – you weren't to know. Blossom's always so cheery about everything. And you're right – Blossom's bakery often looks messy, even when she's on top of things!"

"So how can we help?" Pip asked.

"Well, she's obviously worn out, so I wondered if we could leave her to sleep and finish baking all the cakes. If I gather enough of us, I'm sure we can do it." Catkin looked hopefully at Pip.

Pip frowned. "But she was making so many cakes, and some were brand new recipes!" The little fairy sipped at her tea and thought for a moment. "Wait. I've got an idea! She had a scrapbook in the bakery which had all her cake designs scribbled down – if we can find it, perhaps we *can* finish all the cakes for her!"

Catkin hugged her friend. "That would be wonderful!" she said. "Can you come and help right away? We don't have any time to lose!"

Chapter 5

The two fairies agreed that Pip would go straight to the bakery to find Blossom's scrapbook while Catkin went to gather more fairies to help them. Without Blossom's expert baking skills, they certainly needed more than just the two of them to get all the cakes ready in time! *I'll start with Willa*, Catkin thought to herself. *She's always good in a crisis*. Willa lived next door to Pip in

the opal-oak tree. When Catkin arrived
at the tree, Willa was tiptoeing along an
impossibly narrow branch, her pink wings
tucked away and her arms held out either
side for balance.

"Oh, hi, Catkin." Willa grinned but
didn't move her arms to wave. "I'm
practising for the tightrope competition at
the fête tomorrow. Look, no wings!"

Willa bent her legs and jumped on the branch, landing steadily without even a flutter of her pink wings.

"Wow, that's impressive," said Catkin, hoping that Willa wasn't too busy to help. "Um, Willa, I have a favour to ask. . ."

As soon as she told Willa about Blossom, Willa flew down from the branch and put an arm around Catkin. "Of course!" she cried. "I'm not sure I'll ever be able to bake cakes as well as Blossom can, but I'll certainly try my best!"

Catkin and Willa went to the Tree Palace next, where Princess Primrose lived with the rest of the forest fairy royalty. It was built into an ancient pink diamond-nut tree – a beautiful place with turrets, towers and drawbridges.

The two fairies crept into the palace entrance hall, stepping very carefully to avoid waking anyone who was already sleeping. The trunk of the great tree was hollow, which meant that in the daytime sunshine poured inside it, lighting up the inside of the trunk. Catkin thought it always looked incredible, but now, at night, the sparkling moonlight that shone in looked even more magical.

Catkin tiptoed to the wall and whispered into a forest-fairy-ear-shaped knot in the wood of the entrance hall. Magically, the wall at the knot slid away and transformed into a staircase tunnel. The palace was full of these secret passages, which allowed the fairies to move about the palace quickly and easily. Catkin and Willa stepped inside, and in just a few flutters they arrived outside Primrose's bedroom.

"Primrose, are you awake?" Catkin called gently, listening with her ear pressed against the grand oak door.

"Yes, come in!" Primrose said in a much louder voice.

Willa pushed the door open and the two fairies entered. Primrose's bedroom was a huge circular room with gorgeous leaf-shaped windows. Inside, Primrose was at her dressing table beside her younger sister, Nutmeg. They were painting each other's nails.

"Hello!" called Nutmeg excitedly. "Primrose is painting my nails lime green to match my fancy-dress outfit tomorrow!"

"Hello, Willa, Catkin," Primrose welcomed them. "Is everything all right?"

Primrose blew on her nails as Catkin explained what had happened at the bakery.

"Poor Blossom. . ." Primrose jumped up. "Of course I'll help!"

"Me, too!" joined in Nutmeg.

"Are you sure?" Catkin asked, looking at the pink cuckoo clock on the wall. "Isn't it your bedtime soon?"

Nutmeg's freckly smile broke into a wide grin. "I'm too excited about the fête to sleep! It's OK to come too, isn't it, Primrose?"

Her older sister smiled and nodded. "Just this once!"

Soon, Catkin, Willa, Primrose and Nutmeg were tiptoeing silently into the bakery. Blossom still slept soundly at the counter.

Primrose put her hand to her mouth and her hazel eyes widened. "Oh dear," she whispered. "I see what you mean about there being lots to do!"

Catkin found a duckling-feather blanket and laid it over the sleeping Blossom. Willa carefully lifted her head out of the batter and gently placed it on an ivy-cushion.

Pip's head popped up over the counter – being one of the smallest fairies in Jewel Forest, she could only just see over it if she stood on the tips of her toes. She waved at the fairies and held up Blossom's scrapbook.

"I've found it," she mouthed. Pip cleared the table of cake boxes and the fairies gathered round as she laid the scrapbook down and opened the first page. Together, they looked over Blossom's designs, trying to take everything in.

"Willa, can you put the moonbutter cakes into the oven?" Catkin asked in a soft voice. "And Nutmeg, could you mix together the glow-beam cake ingredients? I think I saw them in a bowl but they need to be blended together." The fairies nodded and began to start work.

"Shall I make the honey and walnut tart?" Primrose mouthed.

"And I can ice the sunshine cake," whispered Pip.

"Yes, please," replied Catkin. "I'll do the

starberry muffins. They're my favourite –
Blossom once let me help her make
them, so I'm hoping I can remember
how. . ."

It wasn't long before the bakery was
filled with scrumptious smells once
more, and the fairies fluttered around,
working as hard and as quickly as

possible to prepare Blossom's creations. Catkin was soon pouring the starberry mixture into muffin tins. "Done!" she said to herself. "Now they're ready for the oven." After carefully placing the tins inside the oven, she closed the door quietly and crossed her fingers. Catkin really hoped these cakes were going to be up to Blossom's high standards. She didn't want to let her – or the fête-goers – down!

Chapter 6

Thankfully,
the forest
birds hadn't
yet begun
their dawn
chorus when
the fairies
tiptoed out
of the bakery.

Catkin pulled the door closed carefully

and smiled as she looked through the window at all the goodies. She couldn't quite believe they'd done it, but the friends had managed to finish every single cake, ready for the fête.

The fairies flew back to their homes to catch up on a little sleep before the fête began. As Catkin drifted off to sleep in her palm-leaf hammock underneath the stars, she wondered what Blossom would think when she woke up!

Blossom slept soundly until dawn, when the tweeting of the birds outside began to stir her from slumber. She opened her eyes, wondering where she was for a moment, and looked down at the duckling-feather blanket covering her. She'd been asleep? *Oh, no!* A wave of sickness rushed over her. Had she accidentally drifted off and left all the cakes half finished?

She leapt up, her heart beating like a drum. She had to blink her green eyes several times before she could believe what she saw. The worktops and tables were filled with stands of magnificent cakes and bulging cake boxes, glowing in the early morning light that shone through the bakery windows.

She clapped a hand to her mouth. *How in fairyland has this happened?* she thought, so shocked she had to hold on to the counter to steady herself. Was it forest fairy magic?

Blossom rushed closer to the cakes and opened one of the boxes that had been tied with moth-silk. Inside were moonbutter cupcakes, perfectly risen and glistening with the sparkly buttercream. Next to the box, on a three-tiered cake stand, were the starberry muffins, and behind those was a box containing the most delicious-looking honey and walnut tart. Then something on the table caught her eye – the bright, magical rays that burst from the edible jewels on the double-layer sunshine cake. It looked even better than she'd imagined!

Blossom jumped as the door opened

suddenly, and Catkin popped her head in.

"Good morning, Blossom, did you sleep well?" Catkin looked around the bakery, a sparkle in her hazel eyes. Blossom guessed she was excited about the fête today – just as she was, now that her cakes were miraculously finished in time!

"Well, yes, thank you, I did." Blossom beamed, thinking how rested and happy she now felt. She opened her mouth to speak but quickly shut it again. Should she mention the magic that had happened in the bakery? Everyone in the forest believed in magic, but she'd never known anything this powerful to happen before – it was a miracle. Blossom didn't want to sound silly in front of sensible Catkin. She might

think she was crazy! But she couldn't
keep something this big a secret – and
Catkin was one of her very best friends.
"Um, Catkin?"

"Yes, Blossom?" Catkin grinned.

"The thing is," Blossom began, "I
didn't do all this. . . I must have fallen
asleep last night, and I was still halfway
through making lots of the cakes. But
when I woke up this morning, there
they were, all ready, as if I'd been
baking all night."

"Really? How strange." Catkin suddenly
felt hot, and guessed her usually pale
cheeks had flushed as red as her hair. She
hoped Blossom hadn't noticed.

"Do you believe that forest fairy magic
could have done something like this?"
Blossom continued. "I just can't think of
any other explanation."

"Well, fairy magic is very strong – especially here in Jewel Forest," Catkin replied, and tried to change the subject. "Would you like a hand taking the cakes down to the fête?"

But Blossom didn't answer. She was staring at Catkin's petal-patchwork skirt.

"Catkin, is that flour on your skirt?"

Catkin looked down and quickly brushed it away.

"Er . . . well. . ." Catkin began, wondering what in fairyland she should say. She looked out of the window for inspiration and spotted some tree squirrels scampering past.

"Oh, look – there's a group of tree squirrels outside on the skyway. Let's ask if they can help us carry some things!"

"Good idea!" Blossom replied, and Catkin let out a sigh of relief.

Soon, the two fairies and the tree squirrels were balancing all the cake stands and boxes as they walked carefully along the walkway towards the fête.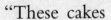

"These cakes smell wonderful!" said Blossom's tree squirrel friend, Sycamore. "I'm going to have to try every single one of them. You won't notice if a box goes missing on the way, will you Blossom. . . ?"

Blossom grinned at Sycamore. "Hey, don't be cheeky!" The tree squirrels were known for their playful nature, but the fairies always kept them in check. "I've counted every single box, and I don't want any disappearing!"

Sycamore pulled a pretend disappointed face, then beamed. "Ah, you know I'm only kidding, Blossom! Your cakes are just so irresistible!"

Chapter 7

Blossom stared in amazement as she flew
along the last section of fairy skyway
and saw the fête spread out below her.
From her bird's-eye view, she could
see garlands in all the colours of the
rainbow hanging on every branch, bush
and toadstool. Fairies fluttered about
between jewel-covered stalls that sparkled
in the sunshine, all offering different
types of entertainment. For refreshments,

as well as Blossom's cake stall, there
was a stall run by the ladybirds from the
Cavern Café, offering different types of
forest tea, a toadstool hut with honey-
floss lollipops, and a jewel-burst popcorn
stand. There were stalls where fairies
and other creatures could have their
nails manicured and painted, a jewellery
stand selling shimmering gems – some
of which Blossom had never even seen
before – and a forest fashion stall with
home-made clothes straight from the
leaf. She hoped she'd get a chance to
check it out later!

But for now, Blossom had to prepare
her own stall, ready for when the fête
opened in just a few moments. She shook
her head as she began setting out the
cake stands and boxes, still wondering
how in fairyland the cakes had all got

finished. She opened the lids for everyone to see the tempting goodies inside, and set the amazing sunshine cake at the centre of the table. She adored baking more than anything else, but displaying her creations was the next best thing – they always looked so pretty, even if she did say so herself!

She heard a loud, booming *dong* – the

signal of the fête being opened – and looked up to see Primrose and Nutmeg smiling at her over the cakes. Her first customers!

"Your cakes look fantastic!" said Primrose. "Can we buy two slices of glow-beam cake, please?"

Blossom nodded. "Of course!" She cut two slices, popped them into a cake box and tied it with spider-silk string.

Primrose opened the box immediately and took a bite of the melt-in-the-mouth cake. It was delicious! Meanwhile Nutmeg passed Blossom a handful of fairy-dust in payment.

As she took the dust, Blossom peered closer at Nutmeg. Did she have a dusting of star sprinkles in her hair? "Nutmeg, what's that in your hair?" she asked.

Primrose swung round to her sister in horror. "Oh, er, you know Nutmeg, she's always messy from her adventures in the forest! Look, Nutmeg, there's the Cavern Café stall – and I'm gasping for a drink. Come on, let's go!" She pulled Nutmeg's hand and they flew away quickly, waving goodbye to Blossom.

Blossom stared at the two fairies flying towards the other side of the fête. Was that moonbutter she could see on the back of Primrose's pink shirt?

But she didn't have time to wonder about it because a long queue had already formed at her cake stall, with many hungry customers desperate to try the delicious-looking cakes. It wasn't just fairies – tree squirrels, hummingbirds, butterflies and bunnies rubbed their hands, legs or paws in glee when they saw the beautiful creations on offer.

Blossom, refreshed from her good night's sleep, worked very hard. Her cakes were selling so quickly that soon there were just two starberry muffins left – and it was only lunchtime! They were snapped up by a pair of purple-speckled toads. *I can't believe I've sold out already*, thought Blossom, looking at the empty cake stands with just a few crumbs remaining.

She began piling up the stands and clearing away the boxes when she heard the tightrope competition being announced.

"Oh, I must go and watch Willa!" Blossom said to herself. She quickly wrote a note on an unused cake box with her beeswax pen and propped it up at the front of her stall: "Sorry, all the cakes are now sold. Thank you for your custom, and happy fête day!" Then she skipped away towards the competition, her pale green wings fluttering with excitement.

In one corner of the fête, in an orange-burst orchard, tightropes were strung up between apple trees. Fairies flew about, eager for the competition to begin. Blossom spotted Primrose and Nutmeg waiting to watch Willa, and she flew over to them.

"So how does the competition work?" Blossom asked Primrose.

The princess explained that the winner would be the first to cross their tightrope without falling off. "But if you use your wings, you're disqualified, and if you fall off, you have to start again!"

Blossom thought it sounded like fun, but when the tree squirrel referee announced the start of the game, she saw just how hard it was! Some of the fairies struggled to balance on the thin silk tightrope, and quickly fell on to the spongy moss floor below.

Willa, however, looked like an expert. She tiptoed across the tightrope as if she was walking along the ground, without so much as a wobble. She had almost reached the other side already, and Blossom held her breath as her friend got close. *Come on, Willa, you can do it!*

Willa took one last step and touched the opposite tree, and the tree squirrel shouted out, "Game over – Willa is the winner!"

Willa bowed as everyone turned to look at her and applaud, and the tree squirrel presented her with a willow-twig hula-hoop as a prize. Her face lit up as she came to join her friends. "Now I can practise something new!" she told them, delighted.

The four fairies flew over to the tea stall. Blossom chose a cherry and wildflower tea, and Willa sipped at a poppy-seed and amber brew. Nutmeg had a sunshine-soak and Primrose had a glitterberry bramble. They all agreed how tasty they were!

"Oh look, there's the tug-of-war!" Blossom noticed suddenly. "Shall we ask to join in?"

Nutmeg and Primrose shook their

heads. "We're going to get some honey-floss lollies. But we'll see you later!"

Willa and Blossom waved to their friends and fluttered over to the tug-of-war. Several fairies stood around the thick moth-silk rope, which was laid out on sandy ground next to a large opal-oak tree. The fairies were divided into two groups – Blossom guessed they were deciding on teams. One of the fairies, with dark cropped hair cut around her pointy ears, called out, "We need one more fairy to even up the teams.

Would anyone like to volunteer?"

Blossom stuck her arm straight up in the air. "Yes, please!" Then she looked at Willa guiltily. "Sorry! Would you mind, Willa – or did you want to have a go?"

Willa shook her head and laughed. "I'm exhausted after the tightrope competition. You go for it!"

·⋅❧ Chapter 8 ❧·⋅·

Blossom was soon in position, at the back of a line of fairies on one side of the tug-of-war.

A tree squirrel stood in the centre, holding up an oak-leaf flag. "On your marks, get ready, GO!" he yelled, bringing down the flag to signal the start of the match.

Blossom held on to the rope tightly, digging her heels into the ground

and fluttering her wings. She tried
her best to pull backwards, but it
was hard work! Instead of pulling the
opposite team over the line marked
in the middle, her team were being
pulled forwards. On the count of three,
Blossom's team heaved on the rope
once more, but it was no good. Her
team fell in a pile, skittering over the
dividing line. The other team had won!

The winning fairies raised their hands
and cheered, but Blossom didn't mind –
it had been good fun, anyway. And
she should probably stick to what she

did best — baking cakes!

While the winning team enjoyed their prizes — acorns filled with rosehip chocolate — Blossom rejoined Willa, and they flew off to find Catkin, Primrose, Pip and Nutmeg.

"Look, there they are." Willa pointed at a stall where a spider tore out tickets from a tulip-petal book.

"It's the raffle!" Blossom realized. "Let's buy a ticket."

They joined their fairy friends at the back of the queue, and soon they all clutched different-coloured tickets.

"The special prize is top secret," Nutmeg told them. "I'm hoping it will be an Olympic-sized trampoline!"

Primrose laughed. "But where would you put that in the palace?"

Just then someone coughed into the

bellflower microphone that stood on the stage in the centre of the fête. "Please gather at the honeysuckle stage for the fancy-dress competition – which will be followed by the forest raffle draw!"

Pip and Nutmeg ran off to change into their fancy-dress outfits, while the other fairies sat on blue-and-white dotted toadstools in front of the stage, chattering about what they'd been doing that day.

"It's been a wonderful fête," said Primrose. "But everyone agrees that your cakes, Blossom, were the very best thing about it!" Their conversation was interrupted as the fancy-dress parade began. Each entrant fluttered, walked or crawled on to the stage in turn. There was a fairy dressed as a daisy chain, a spider wearing a glittering star outfit, a butterfly in a peacock-feather dress, and even a group of ants dressed up as acorns. Nutmeg wore a brilliant bright green parakeet costume, and Pip looked incredible in a blackberry outfit made of real berries. You could pick off the blackberry pips and eat them!

The crowd had to clap for whoever they wanted to win. No one was surprised when Pip received the most cheers, and was awarded with a whole sack of fairy-dust to be spent at Starlight-Starbright tailor's!

Pip beamed at her friends as she joined them on the toadstools, still wearing the berry outfit and offering out pieces of the berry to munch on. Nutmeg ran over too, grinning in her bright green costume, the beaked head nodding up and down. "Pip, you SO deserved to win! Well done!"

"Thanks, Nutmeg," said Pip in her little voice. "I'm sorry I beat you."

Nutmeg readjusted her tail feather and shook her parakeet head. "Don't be silly – I don't mind at all. I just love to dress up!"

Next came the raffle, with lots of exciting prizes. A tree squirrel announced each one in turn, holding up

the colour of the winning tulip petal
for each item. The friends watched as a
hummingbird won
a sapphire
teapot, a
firefly won
a dandelion-
seed blanket, and Primrose
won a diamond-shaped hand mirror –
"Perfect for my bedroom!" she said.

Blossom wasn't too disappointed when
her number didn't come up. She looked
down at her pale turquoise tulip-petal
ticket and smiled at Pip beside her. "I
never was very lucky!" she said.

"But there's one raffle prize left," Pip
said. "It's the extra-special secret prize!
You never know. . ."

"And the winning petal is . . . pale
turquoise!" announced the tree squirrel on

stage as he held up the chosen petal.

Blossom looked down at her petal, then back up at the tree squirrel. It was her ticket! She flew up to the stage, her heart beating fast. The squirrel passed her a golden envelope. "Open it!" he said with a wink.

Blossom slid her finger under the gold flap and took out the piece of sycamore-leaf paper inside. Her hands shook as she read it out:

"CONGRATULATIONS! You have won a party on Shimmer Island – for you and five friends!"

Blossom squealed with excitement. She'd never guessed it would be such a wonderful prize! Shimmer Island was a beautiful place, with beaches fringed with fairy palm trees and shimmering crystal sand.

"Who will you take with you?" the tree squirrel asked.

Blossom didn't have to think twice about that. "My five best fairy friends – Catkin, Pip, Willa, Primrose and Nutmeg. As a thank you to them for finishing all the cakes so beautifully!" She turned to look at the five fairies. Their mouths all gaped open in surprise.

Blossom grinned and flew back down to her friends clutching the golden envelope.

"How did you work it out?" Willa asked.

"I really thought it was fairy magic at first," Blossom replied. "But then I saw the flour on Catkin's skirt, the star sprinkles in Nutmeg's hair, and moonbutter on Primrose's shirt, and I put two and two together!"

Blossom flung her arms around each of her friends in turn, her pale green wings flapping with delight. "And look," she said as she hugged Pip, "there's icing all over your ear!" She brushed it from Pip's pointy ear and chuckled. "I can't believe you all did that for me. It was the loveliest thing ever."

"Well, we saw how tired you looked and couldn't bear to wake you up," said

Catkin. "So we worked as a team to finish all the cakes." Catkin bit her lip. "I do hope they were all OK – we used your scrapbook for the recipes and designs, but none of us are half as good a baker as you are!"

"They were fairytastic," said Blossom. "Everybody loved them." Blossom reached into her bag and pulled out a cake box. Inside were six moonbutter cupcakes. "Actually, we can try some right now – I saved these for us all!" She handed the cakes around, then took the last one and bit into it. The cream icing oozed out. It tasted like the smoothest, silkiest cake ever – just like the ones she'd practised herself. "Yup – they're perfect!" she reassured them all.

As she finished the delicious cake, Blossom blinked back tears of happiness.

She was so lucky to have such wonderful friends. She couldn't think of anyone else she'd rather share her prize party with. It had been the most amazing fête day – all thanks to her forest fairy helpers!

If you enjoyed this

Fashion Fairy Princess

book then why not visit our
magical new website!

- Explore the enchanted world of
the fashion fairy princesses
- Find out which fairy princess
you are
- Download sparkly screensavers
- Make your own tiara
- Colour in your own picture frame
and much more!

fashionfairyprincess.com

Turn the page for a sneak peek of the next
Fashion Fairy Princess adventure...

Chapter 1

Catkin fluttered along a high branch of the sapphire-sycamore tree. The tree leaves shone in the early morning sunshine and Catkin couldn't help but spin in delight as she took in the beautiful forest. "I'm so lucky to live here," she said to herself. She loved Jewel Forest more than anything else, and flying around it always made her happy.

She skipped on to the fairy skyway, a network of glittering bridges that connected the forest houses, shops and palace. Each spring the forest fairies rebuilt the bridges with new leaves. In fact, it was only last week that Catkin had been part of the skyway building team. It had been hard work, but worth all the effort. The skyway was decorated with all sorts of different-coloured gems, and Catkin thought it looked better than any other year!

As she flew along, she pulled out her to-do list of fairy errands from her ivy-leaf trouser pocket.

Buy starberry muffins from Blossom's bakery ✔
Hand out sycamore flyers
Glowberry candles

On Catkin's shoulder was a bag full of sycamore seeds. But these weren't just any sycamore seeds. They were extra-special seeds that she'd collected from the very tree she lived in – the sapphire sycamore. Not only did each winged seed have a sapphire at its centre, but with a sprinkling of fairy magic, the seeds could be sent anywhere in Jewel Forest. Catkin had the idea to use them as a new forest messaging service. When they arrived at their destination, they would spin a short message from the sender in the air. Catkin thought it would be a great way to send instant messages around the forest – quicker than fairy-mail! Today her plan was to hand out the seeds so the fairies and creatures of the forest could see them in action.

She also needed to pick up glowberry

candles for this evening's Walk in the Woods. Catkin had arranged the walk to celebrate the beauty of the forest, and planned to show everyone all the amazing things that grew there. She fluttered along the skyway and spotted the Cavern Café up ahead. *First I'll stop in for a drink*, she thought. All these chores were thirsty work!

The Cavern Café was set inside a large, hollowed-out branch of an opal-oak tree. It ran almost the whole length of the branch, and was sheltered from wind and rain but open to sunshine and the fresh forest air.

"Hello!" Catkin called out as she fluttered into the café. "My usual, please," she said to the waitress, a ladybird named Poppet. Catkin fluttered up to her favourite spot in the café – a terrace along the top of the branch where she could sit and look out at the forest. She sat down at an acorn-nut table and took out her list again. She began adding things with a beeswax pen when Poppet flew up in front of her.

"I'm dreadfully sorry," Poppet squeaked in her high-pitched ladybird voice, "but we've run out of dandelion milkshake. Can I get you a different flavour, Catkin? How about honey-pear? Or carrot and raspberry?"

Catkin frowned. She didn't fancy anything else. The dandelion milkshake always quenched her thirst more than anything else, and it was super-tasty too – sweet and creamy but not too filling. She shook her head, making her red curly hair bounce around her. "I think I'll give it a miss, but thanks, Poppet."

"You could try again tomorrow,"

Poppet suggested. "The problem is we couldn't find a single dandelion in the usual clearing today, but I'm hoping some will grow overnight."

Poppet was right – the magical forest often grew plants very quickly, but it was strange that not one dandelion could be found. Catkin popped her to-do list and pen back in her pocket and fluttered up from the chair. "Thanks, Poppet." The fairy knew that it wasn't just *her* favourite milkshake but one of the café's bestsellers. Many of the fairies and forest creatures would be disappointed that it was off the menu.

Catkin pulled out a sapphire-sycamore seed from her bag. "Before I go, can I give you one of these? It's the newest form of messaging in the forest – with a sprinkle of fairy-dust, you can send a message almost instantly to anyone in the forest!"

Poppet clapped her two front legs together. "What a great idea! Why don't you leave a pile here and I can tell customers about them?"

"That would be fantastic – thanks, Poppet." Catkin grabbed a handful of the seeds and passed them to the ladybird. "I'd better be off now. I'll keep my fingers crossed you have dandelions back in the café tomorrow!"

Get creative with the fashion fairy princesses in these magical sticker-activity books!